A Christmas Medley

STORIES · CAROLS · CHEER

Edited by
Nick Beilenson

Designed by
Michel Design

PETER PAUPER PRESS, INC.
WHITE PLAINS · NEW YORK

To John, Laurence, and Suzanne

The publishers welcome the comments of readers
about this and other Peter Pauper Press titles. Write to
the above address or call (914) 681-0144.

Contents

Christmas Cheer

 **Christmas Carols**

The Wassail Song

Here we come a-wassailing among the leaves
   so green,
Here we come a-wandering so fair to be seen.

Refrain
Love and joy come to you,
And to you your wassail too,
And God bless you and send you a happy
   New Year,
And God send you a happy New Year.

We are the daily beggars that beg from door
   to door,
But we are neighbors' children whom you
   have seen before.

Refrain

God bless the master of this house, likewise
   the mistress too,
And all the little children around the table go.

Refrain

What Child Is This?

What child is this, Who, laid to rest,
On Mary's lap is sleeping?
Whom angels greet with anthems sweet,
While shepherds watch are keeping?

Refrain
This, this is Christ the King,
Whom shepherds guard and angels sing:
This, this who bring Him love
The Babe, the Son of Mary.

Why lies He in such mean estate
Where ox and ass are feeding?
Good Christian, fear: for sinners here
The silent Word is pleading.
Refrain

So bring Him incense, gold, and myrrh,
Come, peasant, king to own Him;
The King of kings salvation brings,
Let loving hearts enthrone him.
Refrain

Jingle Bells

Dashing through the snow,
In a one-horse open sleigh,
O'er the fields we go,

Laughing all the way;
The bells on bobtail ring,
Making spirits bright,
O what fun it is to sing
A sleighing song tonight!

Jingle bells, jingle bells,
Jingle all the way!
Oh, what fun it is to ride
In a one-horse open sleigh!
Jingle bells, jingle bells,
Jingle all the way!
Oh, what fun it is to ride
In a one-horse open sleigh!

The First Nowell

Nowell, Nowell, Nowell, Nowell,
Born is the King of Israel.

The first Nowell, the angels did say,
Was to certain poor shepherds in fields as
    they lay;
In fields where they lay keeping their sheep,
On a cold winter's night that was so deep.

Nowell, Nowell, Nowell, Nowell,
Born is the King of Israel.
Nowell, Nowell, Nowell.

Come to the Manger

Refrain
Come to the manger, come to the manger,
    come to the stall.
Come to the manger, come to the manger,
    come one and all.
Come to the manger, come to the manger,
    by early morn.
Come to the manger, come to the manger,
    Jesus is born.

Peace on earth, good will toward men,
Sing hallelujah again and again.
Peace on earth, good will toward men,
Sing hallelujah again and again.

Refrain

Come to the manger, come to the manger,
    come joyfully.
Come to the manger, come to the manger,
    Jesus to see.
Come to the manger, come to the manger,
    come through the night.
Come to the manger 'til morning bright.

Come to Bethlehem, come and then
Sing hallelujah again and again.

Hark! The Herald Angels Sing

Hark! the herald angels sing,
"Glory to the newborn King;"
Peace on earth, and mercy mild,
God and sinners reconciled!
Joyful, all ye nations, rise,
Join the triumph of the skies;
With th'angelic hosts proclaim,
"Christ is born in Bethlehem!"

Refrain
Hark! the herald angels sing,
"Glory to the newborn King."

Christ, by highest heaven adored;
Christ, the everlasting Lord;
Late in time behold Him come,
Offspring of the virgin's womb.
Veiled in flesh the Godhead see;
Hail th'Incarnate Deity,
Pleased as man with man to dwell;
Jesus, our Emmanuel.

Refrain

Hail, the heav'n-born Prince of Peace!
Hail, the Sun of Righteousness!

Light and life to all He brings,
Ris'n with healing in His wings;
Mild He lays His glory by,
Born that man no more may die,
Born to raise the sons of earth,
Born to give them second birth.

Refrain

It Came upon the Midnight Clear

It came upon the midnight clear,
That glorious song of old,
From angels bending near the earth
To touch their harps of gold;
"Peace on the earth, good will to men,
From heav'n's all-gracious King."
The world in solemn stillness lay
To hear the angels sing.

Still through the cloven skies they come,
With peaceful wings unfurled,
And still their heav'nly music floats
O'er all the weary world;
Above its sad and lowly plains
They bend on hov'ring wing,
And ever o'er its Babel sounds
The blessed angels sing.

For lo! the days are hast'ning on,
By prophet bards foretold,
When with the ever circling years,
Shall come the age of old,
When Peace shall over all the earth
Its heavenly splendors fling,
And all the world give back the song
Which now the angels sing.

Angels We Have Heard on High

Angels we have heard on high,
Sweetly singing o'er the plains,
And the mountains in reply,
Echoing their joyous strains.
Gloria in excelsis Deo,
Gloria in excelsis Deo.

Shepherds, why this jubilee?
Why your joyous songs prolong?
What the gladsome tidings be
Which inspire your heav'nly song?
Gloria in excelsis Deo,
Gloria in excelsis Deo.

Come to Bethlehem and see
Him whose birth the angels sing;

Come, adore on bended knee,
Christ the Lord, the newborn King.
Gloria in excelsis Deo,
Gloria in excelsis Deo.

O Little Town of Bethlehem

O little town of Bethlehem,
How still we see thee lie!
Above thy deep and dreamless sleep,
The silent stars go by;
Yet in thy dark streets shineth
The everlasting Light;
The hopes and fears of all the years
Are met in thee tonight.

For Christ is born of Mary,
And gathered all above,
While mortals sleep, the angels keep
Their watch of wond'ring love.
O morning stars, together
Proclaim the holy birth,
And praises sing to God the King,
And peace to men on earth!

O holy Child of Bethlehem,
Descend to us, we pray;
Cast out our sin and enter in;

Be born in us today!
We hear the Christmas Angels
The great glad tidings tell;
O come to us, abide with us
Our Lord Emmanuel!

Away in a Manger

Away in a manger,
No crib nor a bed,
The little Lord Jesus
Laid down His sweet head.
The stars in the sky,
Looked down where He lay,
The little Lord Jesus
Asleep on the hay.

The cattle are lowing,
The poor baby wakes,
But little Lord Jesus
No crying He makes.
I love Thee, Lord Jesus,
Look down from the sky,
And sit by my cradle
Till morning is nigh.

Be near me Lord Jesus
I ask Thee to stay

Close by me forever,
And love me I pray,
Bless all the dear children
In Thy tender care
And take us to heaven
To live with Thee there.

Silent Night

Silent night, holy night!
All is calm, all is bright
Round yon Virgin Mother and Child.
Holy Infant so tender and mild,
Sleep in heavenly peace,
Sleep in heavenly peace.

Silent night, holy night!
Shepherds quake at the sight!
Glories stream from heaven afar,
Heav'nly hosts sing Alleluia;
Christ, the Savior, is born,
Christ, the Savior, is born.

Silent night, holy night!
Son of God, love's pure light
Radiant beams from Thy holy face
With the dawn of redeeming grace,
Jesus, Lord, at Thy birth,
Jesus, Lord, at Thy birth.

Ring Christmas Bells

Ring, Ring, Ring, Ring
Refrain
Ring Christmas Bells,
Merrily ring.
Tell all the world
Jesus is King.
Loudly proclaim,
With one accord,
Now happy tale,
Welcome the Lord.

Ring, Ring, Ring, Ring
Ring, Ring, Ring, Ring

Ring Christmas bells,
Sound far and near.
Comfort the young,
Jesus is here.
Herald the news
To all the young,
Tell it to all,
In every tongue.

Ring, Ring, Ring, Ring
Ring, Ring, Ring, Ring

Ring Christmas bells,

Toll all along
Your message sweet
Heal and belong.
Come all ye people
Join in the singing
Real people's story
Told by the ringing.

Christmas bells, Christmas bells
Christmas bells, Christmas bells
Ring, Ring, Ring, Ring
Ring, Ring, Ring, Ring

Refrain
Ringing Christmas Bells!

We Wish You a Merry Christmas

Refrain
We wish you a merry Christmas
We wish you a merry Christmas
We wish you a merry Christmas
And a happy New Year.

Good tidings we bring for you and your kin.
We wish you a Merry Christmas and a happy
    New Year.

Refrain

A Visit from St. Nicholas

'Twas the night before Christmas,
   when all through the house
Not a creature was stirring,
   not even a mouse;
The stockings were hung
   by the chimney with care,
In hopes that St. Nicholas
   soon would be there;

The children were nestled
   all snug in their beds,
While visions of sugar-plums
   danced through their heads;
And Mamma in her 'kerchief,
   and I in my cap,
Had just settled our brains
   for a long winter's nap,

When out on the lawn
   there arose such a clatter,
I sprang from my bed
   to see what was the matter.

21

Away to the window
  I flew like a flash,
Tore open the shutters
  and threw up the sash.

The moon on the breast
  of the new-fallen snow
Gave a lustre of mid-day
  to objects below,
When, what to my wondering
  eyes did appear,
But a miniature sleigh,
  and eight tiny reindeer,

With a little old driver
  so lively and quick,
I knew in a moment
  he must be St. Nick.
More rapid than eagles
  his coursers they came,
And he whistled, and shouted,
  and called them by name:

"Now, Dasher! now, Dancer!
  now, Prancer and Vixen!
On, Comet! on, Cupid!
  on, Donder and Blixen!
To the top of the porch!
  to the top of the wall!

Now dash away! dash away!
  dash away, all!"

As leaves that before
  the wild hurricane fly,
When they meet with an obstacle,
  mount to the sky,
So up to the house-top
  the coursers they flew,
With the sleigh full of toys,
  and St. Nicholas too—

And then in a twinkling,
  I heard on the roof
The prancing and pawing
  of each little hoof.
As I drew in my head,
  and was turning around,
Down the chimney St. Nicholas
  came with a bound.

He was dressed all in fur,
  from his head to his foot,
And his clothes were all tarnished
  with ashes and soot;
A bundle of toys he had
  flung on his back,
And he looked like a peddler
  just opening his pack.

His eyes—how they twinkled!
  his dimples, how merry!
His cheeks were like roses,
  his nose like a cherry!
His droll little mouth
  was drawn up like a bow,
And the beard on his chin
  was as white as the snow;

The stump of a pipe
  he held tight in his teeth,
And the smoke it encircled
  his head like a wreath;
He had a broad face
  and a round little belly
That shook when he laughed,
  like a bowl full of jelly.

He was chubby and plump,
  a right jolly old elf,
And I laughed when I saw him
  in spite of myself;
A wink of his eye and
  a twist of his head
Soon gave me to know
  I had nothing to dread;

He spoke not a word, but
  went straight to his work,

And filled all the stockings;
    then turned with a jerk,
And laying his finger
    aside of his nose,
And giving a nod, up the
    chimney he rose.

He sprang to his sleigh,
    to his team gave a whistle,
And away they all flew
    like the down of a thistle.
But I heard him exclaim
    ere he drove out of sight—
"Happy Christmas to all
    and to all a Good Night!"

CLEMENT CLARKE MOORE

There's More!

There's more, much more to Christmas
    Than candle-light and cheer;
It's the spirit of sweet friendship,
    That brightens all the year;
It's thoughtfulness and kindness,
    It's hope reborn again,
For peace, for understanding
    And for goodwill to men!

ANONYMOUS

Scrooge's Nephew on Christmas

"There are many things from which I might
have derived good, by which I have not
profited, . . . Christmas among the rest. But I
am sure I have always thought of Christmas
time, when it has come round . . . as a good
time; a kind, forgiving, charitable, pleasant
time; the only time I know of, in the long
calendar of the year, when men and women
seem by one consent to open their shut-up
hearts freely, and to think of people below
them as if they really were fellow-passengers
to the grave, and not another race of
creatures bound on other journeys. And
therefore, uncle, though it has never put a
scrap of gold or silver in my pocket, I believe
that it *has* done me good, and *will* do me
good; and I say, God bless it!"

CHARLES DICKENS
A Christmas Carol

Fezziwig's Ball

Old Fezziwig laid down his pen, and looked
up at the clock, which pointed to the hour of
seven. He rubbed his hands; adjusted his
capacious waistcoat; laughed all over himself,
from his shoes to his organ of benevolence;

and called out in a comfortable, oily, rich, fat, jovial voice:

"Yo ho, there! Ebenezer! Dick!"

Scrooge's former self, now grown a young man, came briskly in, accompanied by his fellow-'prentice.

"Dick Wilkins, to be sure!" said Scrooge to the Ghost. "Bless me, yes. There he is. He was very much attached to me, was Dick. Poor Dick! Dear, dear!"

"Yo ho, my boys!" said Fezziwig, "no more work tonight. Christmas Eve, Dick! Christmas, Ebenezer! Let's have the shutters up," cried old Fezziwig, with a sharp clap of his hands, "before a man can say Jack Robinson!"

You wouldn't believe how those two fellows went at it! They charged into the street with the shutters—one, two, three—had 'em up in their places—four, five, six—barred 'em and pinned 'em—seven, eight, nine—and came back before you could have got to twelve, panting like race-horses.

"Hilli-ho!" cried old Fezziwig, skipping down from the high desk, with wonderful agility. "Clear away, my lads, and let's have lots of room here! Hilli-ho, Dick! Chirrup, Ebenezer!"

Clear away! There was nothing they wouldn't have cleared away, or couldn't have cleared away, with old Fezziwig looking on.

27

It was done in a minute. Every movable was packed off, as if it were dismissed from public life forevermore; the floor was swept and watered, the lamps were trimmed, fuel was heaped upon the fire; and the warehouse was as snug, and warm, and dry, and bright a ball-room, as you would desire to see upon a winter's night.

In came a fiddler with a music-book, and went up to the lofty desk, and made an orchestra of it, and tuned like fifty stomachaches. In came Mrs. Fezziwig, one vast substantial smile. In came the three Miss Fezziwigs, beaming and lovable. In came the six young followers whose hearts they broke. In came all the young men and women employed in the business. In came the housemaid, with her cousin, the baker. In came the cook, with her brother's particular friend, the milkman. In came the boy from over the way, who was suspected of not having board enough from his master, trying to hide himself behind the girl from next door but one, who was proved to have had her ears pulled by her mistress. In they all came, one after another, some shyly, some boldly, some gracefully, some awkwardly, some pushing, some pulling; in they all came, anyhow and everyhow. Away they all went, twenty couple at once; hands half round and back again the other way; down the middle

and up again; round and round in various stages of affectionate grouping; old top couple always turning up in the wrong place; new top couple starting off again, as soon as they got there; all top couples at last, and not a bottom one to help them!

When this result was brought about, old Fezziwig, clapping his hands to stop the dance, cried out, "Well done!" and the fiddler plunged his hot face into a pot of porter, especially provided for that purpose. But scorning rest upon his reappearance, he instantly began again, though there were no dancers yet, as if the other fiddler had been carried home, exhausted, on a shutter, and he were a bran-new man resolved to beat him out of sight, or perish.

There were more dances, and there were forfeits, and more dances, and there was cake, and there was negus, and there was a great piece of Cold Roast, and there was a great piece of Cold Boiled, and there were mincepies, and plenty of beer. But the great effect of the evening came after the Roast and Boiled when the fiddler (an artful dog, mind! the sort of man who knew his business better than you or I could have told it him!) struck up "Sir Roger de Coverley." Then old Fezziwig stood out to dance with Mrs. Fezziwig. Top couple, too; with a good stiff

piece of work cut out for them; three or four
and twenty pair of partners; people who
were not to be trifled with; people who
would dance, and had no notion of walking.

But if they had been twice as many—ah,
four times—old Fezziwig would have been a
match for them, and so would Mrs. Fezziwig.
As to *her,* she was worthy to be his partner
in every sense of the term. If that's not high
praise, tell me higher, and I'll use it. A
positive light appeared to issue from
Fezziwig's calves. They shone in every part of
the dance like moons. You couldn't have
predicted, at any given time, what would
become of them next. And when old
Fezziwig and Mrs. Fezziwig had gone all
through the dance; advance and retire, both
hands to your partner, bow and curtsey,
corkscrew, thread-the-needle, and back again
to your place, Fezziwig "cut"—cut so deftly,
that he appeared to wink with his legs, and
came upon his feet again without a stagger.

When the clock struck eleven, this
domestic ball broke up. Mr. and Mrs.
Fezziwig took their stations, one on either
side the door, and shaking hands with every
person individually as he or she went out,
wished him or her a Merry Christmas.

CHARLES DICKENS
A Christmas Carol

Yes, Virginia, There Is a Santa Claus

Dear Editor:
I am 8 years old.

Some of my little friends say there is no Santa Claus.

Papa says "If you see it in *The Sun* it's so."

Please tell me the truth: is there a Santa Claus?

VIRGINIA O'HANLON

Virginia, your little friends are wrong. They have been affected by the skepticism of a skeptical age. They do not believe except they see. They think that nothing can be which is not comprehensible by their little minds. All minds, Virginia, whether they be men's or children's, are little. In this great universe of ours man is a mere insect, an ant, in his intellect, as compared with the boundless world about him, as measured by the intelligence capable of grasping the whole of truth and knowledge.

Yes, Virginia, there is a Santa Claus. He exists as certainly as love and generosity and devotion exist, and you know that they abound and give to your life its highest beauty and joy. Alas! how dreary would be the world if there were no Santa Claus! It would be as dreary as if there were no Virginias. There would be no childlike faith then, no poetry, no romance to make tolerable this existence. We should have no enjoyment, except in sense and sight. The eternal light with which childhood fills the world would be extinguished.

Not believe in Santa Claus! You might as well not believe in fairies! You might get your papa to hire men to watch in all the chimneys on Christmas Eve to catch Santa Claus, but even if they did not see Santa Claus coming down, what would that prove? Nobody sees Santa Claus, but that is no sign that there is no Santa Claus. The most real things in the world are those that neither children nor men can see.

No Santa Claus! Thank God, he lives, and he lives forever. A thousand years from now, Virginia, nay, ten times ten thousand years from now, he will continue to make glad the heart of childhood.

FRANCIS P. CHURCH
The New York Sun, *September 21, 1897*

The Gift of the Magi

One dollar and eighty-seven cents. That was all. And sixty cents of it was in pennies. Pennies saved one and two at a time by bulldozing the grocer and the vegetable man and the butcher until one's cheeks burned with the silent imputation of parsimony that such close dealing implied. Three times Della counted it. One dollar and eighty-seven cents. And the next day would be Christmas.

There was clearly nothing to do but flop down on the shabby little couch and howl. So Della did it. Which instigates the moral reflection that life is made up of sobs, sniffles, and smiles, with sniffles predominating.

While the mistress of the home is gradually subsiding from the first stage to the second, take a look at the home. A furnished flat at $8 per week. It did not exactly beggar description, but it certainly had that word on the lookout for the mendicancy squad.

In the vestibule below was a letter-box into which no letter would go, and an electric button from which no mortal finger could coax a ring. Also appertaining thereunto was a card bearing the name "Mr. James Dillingham Young."

The "Dillingham" had been flung to the breeze during a former period of prosperity when its possessor was being paid $30 per week. Now, when the income was shrunk to $20, the letters of "Dillingham" looked blurred, as though they were thinking seriously of contracting to a modest and unassuming D. But whenever Mr. James Dillingham Young came home and reached his flat above he was called "Jim" and greatly hugged by Mrs. James Dillingham Young, already introduced to you as Della. Which is all very good.

Della finished her cry and attended to her cheeks with the powder rag. She stood by the window and looked out dully at a grey cat walking a grey fence in a grey backyard. Tomorrow would be Christmas Day, and she had only $1.87 with which to buy Jim a present. She had been saving every penny she could for months, with this result. Twenty dollars a week doesn't go far. Expenses had been greater than she had calculated. They always are. Only $1.87 to buy a present for Jim. Her Jim. Many a happy hour she had spent planning for something nice for him. Something fine and rare and sterling— something just a little bit near to being worthy of the honour of being owned by Jim.

There was a pier-glass between the windows of the room. Perhaps you have seen a pier-glass in an $8 flat. A very thin and very agile person may, by observing his reflection in a rapid sequence of longitudinal strips, obtain a fairly accurate conception of his looks. Della, being slender, had mastered the art.

Suddenly she whirled from the window and stood before the glass. Her eyes were shining brilliantly, but her face had lost its colour within twenty seconds. Rapidly she pulled down her hair and let it fall to its full length.

Now, there were two possessions of the James Dillingham Youngs in which they both took a mighty pride. One was Jim's gold watch that had been his father's and grandfather's. The other was Della's hair. Had the Queen of Sheba lived in the flat across the airshaft, Della would have let her hair hang out the window some day to dry just to depreciate Her Majesty's jewels and gifts. Had King Solomon been the janitor, with all his treasures piled up in the basement, Jim would have pulled out his watch every time he passed, just to see him pluck at his beard from envy.

So now Della's beautiful hair fell about her,

rippling and shining like a cascade of brown
waters. It reached below her knee and made
itself almost a garment for her. And then she
did it up again nervously and quickly. Once
she faltered for a minute and stood still while
a tear or two splashed on the worn red
carpet.

On went her old brown jacket; on went
her old brown hat. With a whirl of skirts and
with the brilliant sparkle still in her eyes, she
fluttered out the door and down the stairs to
the street.

Where she stopped the sign read: "Mme.
Sofronie. Hair Goods of All Kinds." One flight
up Della ran, and collected herself, panting.
Madame, large, too white, chilly, hardly
looked the "Sofronie."

"Will you buy my hair?" asked Della.

"I buy hair," said Madame. "Take yer hat off
and let's have a sight at the looks of it."

Down rippled the brown cascade.

"Twenty dollars," said Madame, lifting the
mass with a practised hand.

"Give it to me quick," said Della.

Oh, and the next two hours tripped by on
rosy wings. Forget the hashed metaphor. She
was ransacking the stores for Jim's present.

She found it at last. It surely had been
made for Jim and no one else. There was no

other like it in any of the stores, and she had turned all of them inside out. It was a platinum fob chain simple and chaste in design, properly proclaiming its value by substance alone and not by meretricious ornamentation—as all good things should do. It was even worthy of The Watch. As soon as she saw it she knew that it must be Jim's. It was like him. Quietness and value—the description applied to both. Twenty-one dollars they took from her for it, and she hurried home with the 87 cents. With that chain on his watch Jim might be properly anxious about the time in any company. Grand as the watch was, he sometimes looked at it on the sly on account of the old leather strap that he used in place of a chain.

When Della reached home her intoxication gave way a little to prudence and reason. She got out her curling irons and lighted the gas and went to work repairing the ravages made by generosity added to love. Which is always a tremendous task, dear friends—a mammoth task.

Within forty minutes her head was covered with tiny close-lying curls that made her look wonderfully like a truant schoolboy. She looked at her reflection in the mirror long, carefully, and critically.

"If Jim doesn't kill me," she said to herself, "before he takes a second look at me, he'll say I look like a Coney Island chorus girl. But what could I do—oh! what could I do with a dollar and eighty-seven cents?"

At 7 o'clock the coffee was made and the frying-pan was on the back of the stove hot and ready to cook the chops.

Jim was never late. Della doubled the fob chain in her hand and sat on the corner of the table near the door that he always entered. Then she heard his step on the stair away down on the first flight, and she turned white for just a moment. She had a habit of saying little silent prayers about the simplest everyday things, and now she whispered: "Please God, make him think I am still pretty."

The door opened and Jim stepped in and closed it. He looked thin and very serious. Poor fellow, he was only twenty-two—and to be burdened with a family! He needed a new overcoat and he was without gloves.

Jim stopped inside the door, as immovable as a setter at the scent of quail. His eyes were fixed upon Della, and there was an expression in them that she could not read, and it terrified her. It was not anger, nor surprise, nor disapproval, nor horror, nor any

of the sentiments that she had been prepared for. He simply stared at her fixedly with that peculiar expression on his face.

Della wriggled off the table and went for him.

"Jim, darling," she cried, "don't look at me that way. I had my hair cut off and sold it because I couldn't have lived through Christmas without giving you a present. It'll grow out again—you won't mind, will you? I just had to do it. My hair grows awfully fast. Say 'Merry Christmas!' Jim, and let's be happy. You don't know what a nice—what a beautiful, nice gift I've got for you."

"You've cut off your hair?" asked Jim, laboriously, as if he had not arrived at that patent fact yet even after the hardest mental labour.

"Cut it off and sold it," said Della. "Don't you like me just as well, anyhow? I'm me without my hair, ain't I?"

Jim looked about the room curiously.

"You say your hair is gone?" he said, with an air almost of idiocy.

"You needn't look for it," said Della. "It's sold, I tell you—sold and gone, too. It's Christmas Eve, boy. Be good to me, for it went for you. Maybe the hairs of my head were numbered," she went on with a sudden serious sweetness, "but nobody could ever count my love for you. Shall I put the chops on, Jim?"

Out of his trance Jim seemed quickly to wake. He enfolded his Della. For ten seconds let us regard with discreet scrutiny some inconsequential object in the other direction. Eight dollars a week or a million a year—what is the difference? A mathematician or a wit would give you the wrong answer. The magi brought valuable gifts, but that was not among them. This dark assertion will be illuminated later on.

Jim drew a package from his overcoat pocket and threw it upon the table.

"Don't make any mistake, Dell," he said, "about me. I don't think there's anything in the way of a haircut or a shave or a shampoo that could make me like my girl any less. But if you'll unwrap that package you may see why you had me going a while at first."

White fingers and nimble tore at the string and paper. And then an ecstatic scream of joy; and then, alas! a quick feminine change to hysterical tears and wails, necessitating the immediate employment of all the comforting powers of the lord of the flat.

For there lay The Combs—the set of combs, side and back, that Della had worshipped for long in a Broadway window. Beautiful combs, pure tortoise shell, with jeweled rims—just the shade to wear in the beautiful vanished hair. They were expensive combs, she knew, and her heart had simply craved and yearned over them without the least hope of possession. And now, they were hers, but the tresses that should have adorned the coveted adornments were gone.

But she hugged them to her bosom, and at length she was able to look up with dim eyes and a smile and say: "My hair grows so fast, Jim!"

And then Della leaped up like a little singed cat and cried, "Oh, oh!"

Jim had not yet seen his beautiful present. She held it out to him eagerly upon her open palm. The dull precious metal seemed to flash with a reflection of her bright and ardent spirit.

"Isn't it a dandy, Jim? I hunted all over town to find it. You'll have to look at the time a hundred times a day now. Give me your watch. I want to see how it looks on it."

Instead of obeying, Jim tumbled down on the couch and put his hands under the back of his head and smiled.

"Dell," said he, "let's put our Christmas presents away and keep 'em a while. They're

43

too nice to use just at present. I sold the watch to get the money to buy your combs. And now suppose you put the chops on."

The magi, as you know, were wise men—wonderfully wise men who brought gifts to the Babe in the manger. They invented the art of giving Christmas presents. Being wise, their gifts were no doubt wise ones, possibly bearing the privilege of exchange in case of duplication. And here I have lamely related to you the uneventful chronicle of two foolish children in a flat who most unwisely sacrificed for each other the greatest treasures of their house. But in a last word to the wise of these days let it be said that of all who give gifts these two were the wisest. Of all who give and receive gifts, such as they are wisest. Everywhere they are wisest. They are the magi.

O. HENRY

The Selfish Giant

Every afternoon, as they were coming from school, the children used to go and play in the Giant's garden.

It was a large lovely garden, with soft green grass. Here and there over the grass stood beautiful flowers like stars, and there

44

were twelve peach-trees that in the springtime broke out into delicate blossoms of pink and pearl, and in the autumn bore rich fruit. The birds sat on the trees and sang so sweetly that the children used to stop their games in order to listen to them. "How happy we are here!" they cried to each other.

One day the Giant came back. He had been to visit his friend the Cornish ogre, and had stayed with him for seven years. After the seven years were over he had said all that he had to say, for his conversation was limited, and he determined to return to his own castle. When he arrived he saw the children playing in the garden.

"What are you doing there?" he cried in a very gruff voice, and the children ran away.

"My own garden is my own garden," said the Giant; "anyone can understand that, and I will allow nobody to play in it but myself." So he built a high wall all round it, and put up a notice-board:

TRESPASSERS
WILL BE
PROSECUTED

He was a very selfish giant.

The poor children had now nowhere to

play. They tried to play on the road, but the road was very dusty and full of hard stones, and they did not like it. They used to wander round the high wall when their lessons were over, and talk about the beautiful garden inside. "How happy we were there," they said to each other.

Then the spring came, and all over the country there were little blossoms and little birds. Only in the garden of the Selfish Giant it was still winter. The birds did not care to sing in it, as there were no children, and the trees forgot to blossom. Once a beautiful flower put its head out from the grass, but when it saw the notice-board it was so sorry for the children that it slipped back into the ground again, and went off to sleep. The only people who were pleased were the Snow and the Frost. "Spring has forgotten this garden," they cried, "so we will live here all the year round." The Snow covered up the grass with her great white cloak, and the Frost painted all the trees silver. Then they invited the North Wind to stay with them, and he came. He was wrapped in furs, and he roared all day about the garden, and blew the chimney-pots down. "This is a delightful spot," he said; "we must ask the Hail on a visit." So the Hail came. Every day for three hours he rattled on the roof of the castle till he broke most of the slates, and then he ran round and round the garden as fast as he could go. He was dressed in grey, and his breath was like ice.

"I cannot understand why the spring is so late in coming," said the Selfish Giant, as he sat at the window and looked out at his cold white garden; "I hope there will be a change in the weather."

But the spring never came, nor the summer. The autumn gave golden fruit to every garden, but to the Giant's garden she gave none. "He is too selfish," she said. So it was always winter there, and the North Wind, and the Hail, and the Frost, and the Snow danced about through the trees.

One morning the Giant was lying awake in bed when he heard some lovely music. It sounded so sweet to his ears that he thought it must be the King's musicians passing by. It was really only a little linnet singing outside his window, but it was so long since he had heard a bird sing in his garden that it seemed to him to be the most beautiful music in the world. Then the Hail stopped dancing over his head, and the North Wind ceased roaring, and a delicious perfume came to him through the open casement. "I believe the spring has come at last," said the Giant, and he jumped out of bed and looked out.

What did he see?

He saw a most wonderful sight. Through a little hole in the wall the children had crept in, and they were sitting in the branches of the trees. In every tree that he could see there was a litle child. And the trees were so glad to have the children back again that they had covered themselves with blossoms, and were waving their arms gently above the children's heads. The birds were flying about and twittering with delight, and the flowers were looking up through the green grass and laughing. It was a lovely scene, only in one corner it was still winter. It was the farthest corner of the garden, and in it was standing a little boy. He was so small that he could not reach up to the branches of the tree, and he was wandering all round it, crying bitterly. The poor tree was still quite covered with frost and snow, and the North Wind was blowing and roaring above it. "Climb up! little boy," said the Tree, and it bent its branches down as low as it could; but the boy was too tiny.

And the Giant's heart melted as he looked out. "How selfish I have been!" he said; "now I know why the spring would not come here. I will put that poor little boy on the top of the tree, and then I will knock down the wall, and my garden shall be the children's play-ground for ever and ever." He was really very sorry for what he had done.

So he crept down-stairs and opened the front door quite softly, and went out into the garden. But when the children saw him they were so frightened that they all ran away, and the garden became winter again. Only the little boy did not run, for his eyes were so full of tears that he did not see the Giant coming. And the Giant strode up behind him and took him gently in his hand, and put him up into the tree. And the tree broke at once into blossom, and the birds came and sang on it, and the little boy stretched out his two arms and flung them round the Giant's neck, and kissed him. And the other children, when they saw that the Giant was not wicked any longer, came running back, and with them came the spring. "It is your garden now, little children," said the Giant, and he took a great axe and knocked down the wall. And when the people were going to market at twelve o'clock they found the Giant playing with the children in the most beautiful garden they had ever seen.

All day long they played, and in the evening they came to the Giant to bid him good-bye.

"But where is your little companion?" he said, "the boy I put into the tree." The Giant loved him the best because he had kissed him.

"We don't know," answered the children; "he has gone away."

"You must tell him to be sure and come here tomorrow," said the Giant. But the children said that they did not know where he lived, and had never seen him before; and the Giant felt very sad.

Every afternoon, when school was over, the children came and played with the Giant. But the little boy whom the Giant loved was never seen again. The Giant was very kind to all the children, yet he longed for his first little friend, and often spoke of him. "How I would like to see him!" he used to say.

Years went over, and the Giant grew very old and feeble. He could not play about any more, so he sat in a huge armchair, and watched the children at their games, and admired his garden. "I have many beautiful flowers," he said; "but the children are the most beautiful flowers of all."

One winter morning he looked out of his window as he was dressing. He did not hate the winter now, for he knew that it was merely spring asleep, and that the flowers were resting.

Suddenly he rubbed his eyes in wonder, and looked and looked. It certainly was a marvellous sight. In the farthest corner of the garden was a tree quite covered with lovely white blossoms. Its branches were all golden, and silver fruit hung down from them, and underneath it stood the little boy he had loved.

Down-stairs ran the Giant in great joy, and out into the garden. He hastened across, and came near to the child. And when he came quite close his face grew red with anger, and he said, "Who hath dared to wound thee?" For on the palms of the child's hands were the prints of two nails, and the prints of two nails were on the little feet.

"Who hath dared to wound thee?" cried the Giant, "tell me, that I may take my big sword and slay him." "Nay!" answered the child; "but these are the wounds of Love."

"Who art thou?" said the Giant, and a strange awe fell on him, and he knelt before the little child.

And the child smiled on the Giant, and said to him, "You let me play once in your garden; today you shall come with me to my garden, which is Paradise."

And when the children ran in that afternoon, they found the Giant lying dead under the tree, all covered with white blossoms.

OSCAR WILDE

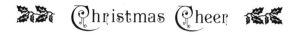

Christmas Cheer

A Tree-Trimming Party Menu

Mulled Cider Punch

Egg Nog

Hot Spiced Cranberry Punch

Christmas Fruit Cake

English Plum Pudding with Hard Sauce

Egg Nog Pie

Mincemeat Pie

Chocolate Roll

Chocolate Mousse

Viennese Yuletide Crescents

Sugar Cookies

Chocolate Almond Crunchies

Mulled Cider Punch

6   quarts cider
2   teaspoons whole cloves
3   sticks cinnamon
½   teaspoon nutmeg
¾   cup sugar

Combine cider, cloves, cinnamon, nutmeg and sugar; bring to boil for 5 minutes; strain. Serve hot.

20 to 25 servings

Egg Nog

8   eggs, separated
6   tablespoons sugar
6   cups milk
     Rum or rum flavoring to taste
2   cups heavy cream
     Nutmeg

Beat together egg yolks and sugar until thick and pale. Stir in milk and rum or rum flavoring. Beat egg whites until stiff. Whip cream. Fold egg whites into egg yolk mixture and fold in whipped cream. Add more sugar if necessary. Pour into punch bowl and sprinkle surface with nutmeg.

10 servings

Hot Spiced Cranberry Punch

¾   cup firmly packed brown sugar
¼   teaspoon salt
¼   teaspoon nutmeg
½   teaspoon cinnamon
½   teaspoon allspice
¾   teaspoon cloves
2   16-ounce cans jellied cranberry sauce
1   quart pineapple juice
    Butter or margarine
    Cinnamon sticks

Bring sugar, 1 cup water, salt, and spices to a boil. Crush cranberry sauce with fork. Add 3 cups water and beat with rotary beater until smooth. Add cranberry liquid and pineapple juice to hot spiced syrup and heat to boiling. Serve hot. Dot with butter or margarine. Serve with cinnamon stick stirrers.

2½ quarts

Christmas Fruit Cake

½   pound chopped candied cherries
¼   pound chopped candied citron
¼   pound chopped walnuts
¼   pound chopped pecans
½   pound raisins
¼   pound lemon peel, cut up
¼   pound orange peel, cut up
1¾ cups all-purpose flour, divided
1   cup butter
½   cup sugar
½   cup honey
5   eggs, beaten
1   teaspoon salt
1   teaspoon baking powder
1   teaspoon allspice
½   teaspoon nutmeg
½   teaspoon cinnamon
½   teaspoon cloves
¼   cup orange or grape juice
    Almonds and cherries to garnish
    (optional)
    Brandy (optional)

Combine candied fruits, nuts, raisins, lemon
and orange peel. Dredge in ¼ cup flour.
Cream butter and sugar; add honey, then
eggs, and beat well. Sift remaining 1½ cups

flour with dry ingredients and add alternately with fruit juice, beating thoroughly. Pour batter over floured fruits and mix well. Line 2 greased 7½-inch x 3½-inch loaf pans with waxed paper, allowing ½ inch to extend above all sides of pans. Pour batter into pans; do not flatten. Put pan holding 2 cups water on bottom shelf of oven. Bake in 250° oven 3 to 4 hours. If decoration of almonds and cherries is used, place on cake at end of 2 hours. If desired, pour brandy over cake and wrap in brandy-soaked cloth. Store in covered container in a cool place.

English Plum Pudding

10   slices white bread
1   cup scalded milk
½   cup sugar
4   eggs, separated
1⅓   cups golden raisins, lightly floured
½   cup finely chopped dates
3   tablespoons finely chopped citron
¾   cup finely chopped suet
3   tablespoons brandy (optional)
1   teaspoon nutmeg
½   teaspoon cinnamon

¼   teaspoon ground cloves
¼   teaspoon mace
1   teaspoon salt

Crumb bread and soak in hot milk. Cool and add sugar, egg yolks, raisins, dates, and citron. Cream suet in food processor and add to crumb mixture. Stir in brandy (if desired), nutmeg, cinnamon, cloves, mace, and salt. Beat until well blended. Beat egg whites until stiff but not dry. Stir a third of the egg whites into pudding mixture; gently fold in the remainder. Spoon mixture into a buttered 2-quart mold and cover. Steam for 6 hours in a large covered pot holding boiling water to come halfway up the sides of the mold. Remove and let cool for 10 minutes before unmolding. Serve with warm hard sauce.

Hard Sauce

5   tablespoons butter
1   cup confectioners sugar
½   teaspoon vanilla

Cream butter, add sugar and beat with electric beater until pale and creamy. Add vanilla and blend. Cover and refrigerate until needed.

Egg Nog Pie

3   eggs, separated
½   cup sugar
2   cups light cream
⅛   teaspoon salt
¼   teaspoon nutmeg
     Rum or rum flavoring to taste
     Pastry dough for 9-inch 1-crust pie
     Slightly sweetened whipped cream
     (optional)
     Candied rinds to garnish

Beat egg yolks, sugar and cream. Add salt,
nutmeg, and rum or rum flavoring. Beat egg
whites until stiff and fold into mixture. Pour
into unbaked pie shell. Bake in 450° oven 10
minutes, then at 325° until firm, about 25
minutes. For a very rich dessert, top with
slightly sweetened whipped cream. Garnish
pie with red and green candy flowers, made
from candied rinds.

Mincemeat Pie

1   can (1⅔ cups) mincemeat
2   cups thinly sliced apples
1   teaspoon grated lemon peel

2   tablespoons lemon juice
      Pastry dough for 9-inch 2-crust pie

Combine mincemeat, apples, lemon peel,
and juice; heat thoroughly. Pour into 9-inch
pastry-lined pie pan; adjust top crust.
Sprinkle with a small amount of sugar and
bake in 400° oven 35 minutes.

Chocolate Roll

5   large eggs, separated
⅔   cup sugar
6   ounces semi-sweet chocolate
3   tablespoons strong coffee
      Cocoa
1¼   cups heavy cream, whipped

Butter 8-inch x 12-inch baking sheet. Line
with waxed paper and butter paper. Beat egg
yolks and sugar with rotary beater or electric
mixer until thick and pale in color.
   Combine chocolate and coffee and place
over low heat in double boiler. Stir until
chocolate melts. Let mixture cool slightly
and stir into egg yolks. Beat egg whites until
stiff and fold in. Spread mixture evenly on

prepared baking sheet and bake 14 minutes in 350° oven, or until knife inserted in middle comes out clean. Do not overbake.

Remove pan from oven and cover cake with a damp cloth. Let stand 30 minutes or until cool. Loosen cake from baking sheet and dust cake generously with cocoa. Turn cake out on wax paper, cocoa side down, and carefully remove paper from bottom of cake. Spread cake with whipped cream, sweetened and flavored to taste, and roll up like a jelly roll. For easy rolling, firmly grasp each corner of wax paper on which cake was turned out and flip over about two inches of edge on top of cake. Continue to roll by further lifting wax paper. The last roll should deposit log on a long platter. Cover top with whipped cream. Garnish with chocolate shavings.

8 servings

Chocolate Mousse

4   ounces semi-sweet chocolate morsels
5   eggs, separated
3   tablespoons sugar
½   pint heavy cream

2   tablespoons brandy (optional)

Melt chocolate morsels in top of double boiler. Put into bowl and add beaten egg yolks. Mix thoroughly. In another bowl add sugar to heavy cream and whip. Add whipped cream to chocolate mixture. Beat egg whites until stiff and fold into chocolate mixture. Add brandy, if desired. Pour into serving bowl and refrigerate for at least 10 hours.

Viennese Yuletide Crescents

1   cup soft butter
⅓   cup granulated sugar
⅔   cup ground almonds
¼   teaspoon salt
1⅔ cups all-purpose flour
      Confectioners sugar

Mix first 4 ingredients together thoroughly—then work in flour with hands. Chill dough. Pull off small pieces of chilled dough and work with hands until pliable but not sticky. Roll between palms into pencil-thick strips and shape into small crescents on ungreased cookie sheets. Bake at 350° until set but not brown (about 15 minutes). Remove from cookie sheets when cooled and roll in confectioners sugar.

75 cookies

Sugar Cookies

½   cup soft butter
½   cup sugar
1   egg
1   tablespoon milk or cream
½   teaspoon vanilla
½   teaspoon lemon extract
1½   cups all-purpose flour
1   teaspoon cream of tartar
½   teaspoon baking soda
¼   teaspoon salt

Combine ingredients in above order. Chill dough. Roll out very thin, about ¹⁄₁₆-inch thick. Cut into fancy shapes with cookie cutters; sprinkle with colored sugar and bake at 400° on greased cookie sheets until very lightly browned—about 5-6 minutes. Watch carefully to keep from over-browning.

About 80 small cookies

Chocolate Almond Crunchies

½   cup butter, softened
1   tablespoon brown sugar
2   tablespoons granulated sugar
1   teaspoon vanilla
½   cup chopped toasted almonds
½   cup miniature chocolate chips
1   cup all-purpose flour
    Confectioners sugar

Combine all ingredients and mix thoroughly. Shape into 1-inch balls. Bake at 350° for 15 minutes. Check after 10 minutes (the bottoms tend to burn). Remove from oven and roll in confectioners sugar while still warm.

36 cookies